The Picture of
Morty & Ray

by DANIEL PINKWATER
illustrated by JACK E. DAVIS

HarperCollins*Publishers*

I am Morty. My friend is Ray.

I stayed over at Ray's house.
We watched the late movie.

It was a scary movie. It was
about a handsome guy who
had his picture painted.

After the picture was painted,
everybody came around to
see it and said it was just as
handsome as he was.

The handsome guy behaved
like a jerk. He went around
being rude and hurting people's
feelings.

He said mean things to people
and played tricks on them.

Like this: He had a flower in his buttonhole. And he said to people, "Smell my flower!" When they got close and ready to sniff the flower, he would make it squirt them with water.

Then he would laugh.

He was a really evil guy.

Or he would tell people, "Look! Your shoe is untied!" They would bend over to tie their shoes, and he would push them over.

Then he would laugh.

He had this cruel laugh.

He would break open pieces of bubble gum and put hot pepper in the middle. He would insist that people put cooking pots on their heads, saying a huge rainstorm was coming. Then he would squirt them.

So, as I was saying, he had his picture painted, and everybody came to see it and make a big fuss about it. Even though he was cruel, he had a lot of friends because he was rich and threw a lot of parties.

Only somebody noticed
that the picture was
looking a little bit ugly.
The rich handsome guy
looked handsome as
ever, but the picture had
changed!

This is where the movie really got good! Every time the guy did something mean, the picture would get a little uglier.

So he put it in a closet, where no one would see it.

He continued to do bad things.

At the end of the movie, the guy has done rotten things for his whole life, and he still looks nice and handsome.

Then we get to see the picture. It is gruesome! It is gross! It is ugly! It is awful and disgusting!

"Neat!" I shouted.

"Neat!" Ray shouted. "It is a neat movie!"

"Did you see what a neat picture?"

"Neat!"

"Let's do one, Morty!"

"Yes!"

"You paint me, and I'll paint you!"

"Right!"

"Get the paints!"

We painted a picture. We were both in it. I painted Ray and Ray painted me. We tried to paint each other as handsome as we could.

"The picture is good," Ray said.

"Yep. It is good," I said. "We are good painters."

"Now we have to do rotten things and see if the picture gets uglier."

"Do you think it will?" I asked Ray.

"We won't know until we try. It's an experiment."

At school we pushed little kids in the hall. We spat chewed gum in the water fountain. We stopped up the toilets with big wads of toilet paper.

After school we looked at the picture.

"I think it's a little uglier," I said.

"Maybe," Ray said. "Maybe just a little uglier. I'm not sure."

The next day, on the
school bus, we stuck our
butts out the window. We
stamped on somebody's
lunch. In the lunchroom we
spilled chocolate milk all over.

And we called people
names. We called them
Lard Head, Bubble Butt,
Banana Nose, Four Eyes,
Jelly Belly, Beanpole,
Smelly Nelly, and
Garbage Breath.

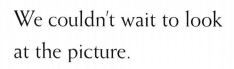

We couldn't wait to look at the picture.

"It worked!" Ray said. "Look! It's uglier!"

"Yaaay!" we shouted.

The next day we took the last two pickles out of a big pickle jar and stuffed them into our friend Oscar's pants. Then we poured the pickle juice on him and told people he had wet himself.

Oscar got mad. "I will never speak to you again," he said.

"Why?" we asked Oscar. "Why will you never speak to us again?"

"I thought you were my friends," Oscar said.

"We are. We were just trying to get our picture to turn ugly."

"Your picture?"

"Shall we show him?" I asked Ray.

"Yes. Let's show him," Ray said.

LOCKER N°
202

We showed Oscar the picture.
It was lots uglier.

"Ooo!" I said. "This is maybe
a little too ugly."

"It's pretty ugly," Ray said. "I'm
nauseated."

Neat!" Oscar said. "Neat, neat,
neat! This is the coolest thing
I have ever seen!"

"You like it?" we asked Oscar.

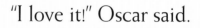

"I love it!" Oscar said.

"You can have it," Ray said. "We're starting to get disgusted with it."

"Cool!" Oscar said.

"He likes the picture," I said.

"Go figure," Ray said.

"I guess different people like different things," I said.

"Right," Ray said. "Let's go and drink some pickle juice."

For Jill—picture perfect in
the best possible way—D.P.

For Cathy—J.E.D.

The Picture of Morty & Ray
Text copyright © 2003 by Daniel Pinkwater
Illustrations copyright © 2003 by Jack E. Davis
Printed in the U.S.A. All rights reserved.
www.harperchildrens.com

Library of Congress Cataloging-in-Publication Data
Pinkwater, Daniel Manus, date.
The picture of Morty & Ray / by Daniel Pinkwater ; illustrated by Jack E. Davis.
p.   cm.
Summary: Inspired by a movie plot, Morty and Ray paint pictures of each other
and then do mean things at school to see if their portraits will become ugly.
ISBN 0-06-623785-8 — ISBN 0-06-623786-6 (lib. bdg.)
[1. Portraits—Fiction.   2. Conduct of life—Fiction.   3. Humorous stories.]
I. Davis, Jack E., ill.   II. Title.
PZ7.P6335 Pk   2003   [E]—dc21   2002020533

Typography by Stephanie Bart-Horvath
1 2 3 4 5 6 7 8 9 10
❖
First Edition